for Mom and Dad

THIS IS A BORZOI BOOK PUBLISHED BY ALFRED A. KNOPF

Copyright © 2009 by Susan Gal
All rights reserved. Published in the United States by Alfred A. Knopf,
an imprint of Random House Children's Books, a division of
Random House, Inc., New York.

Knopf, Borzoi Books, and the colophon are registered trademarks
of Random House, Inc.

Visit us on the Web! www.randomhouse.com/kids
Educators and librarians, for a variety of teaching tools, visit us at
www.randomhouse.com/teachers

Library of Congress Cataloging-in-Publication Data
Gal, Susan.
Night lights / Susan Gal. — 1st ed.
p. cm.
Summary: While preparing for bedtime, a little girl and her dog note all
the different kinds of lights that brighten up the night, from headlights
to moonlight.
ISBN 978-0-375-85862-8 (trade) — ISBN 978-0-375-95862-5 (lib. bdg.)
[1. Night—Fiction. 2. Light—Fiction.] I. Title.
PZ7.G12964Ni 2009
[Fic]—dc22
2008050909

The illustrations in this book were created using
charcoal on paper and digital collage.

MANUFACTURED IN CHINA
November 2009
10 9 8 7 6 5 4 3 2 1

First Edition

Night Lights

by Susan Gal

Alfred A. Knopf

New York

streetlight

headlight

porch light

lantern light

firelight

candlelight

firefly light

lightning!

bathroom light

reading light

flashlight

spotlight

night-light

moonlight

starlight

good night